# ZUBIE the Lightning Bug

## I Want To Remember Your Thoughts

~This book is dedicated to ~
Austen, Kaden and Bailee

"Psst...up here...
My name is Zubie, I'm
special because my tail
lights up the summer
night."

"I want to share my story with you,
one day my mom asked, "Zubie,
some people call us fire flies,  some
call us lightning bugs and others
call us glow bugs. "

"Which do you prefer to be called?"

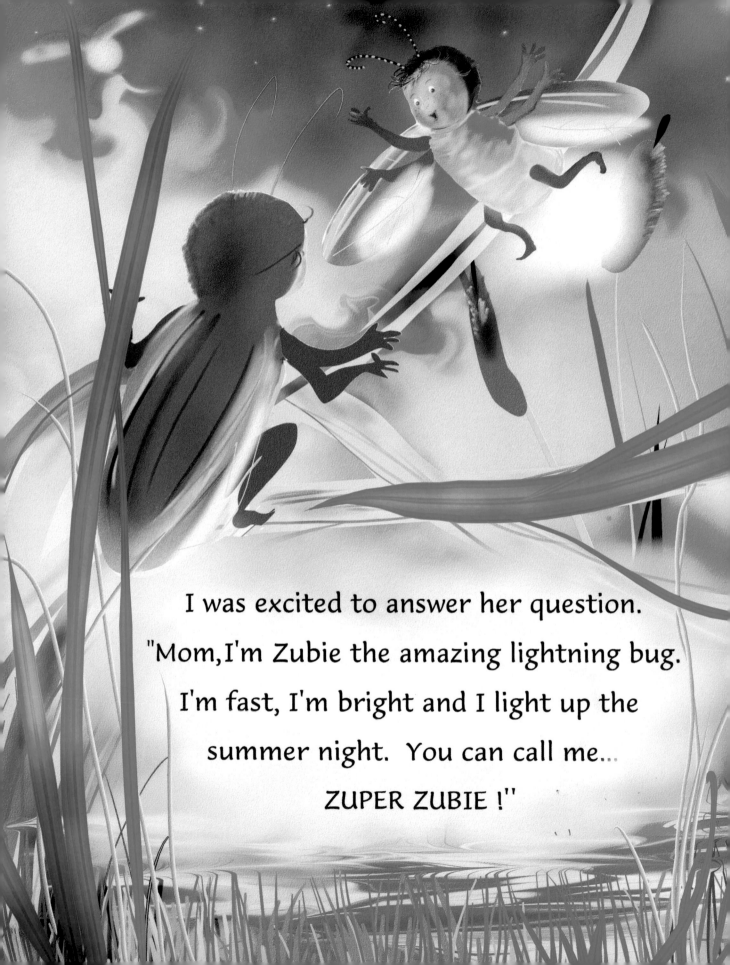

I was excited to answer her question.
"Mom, I'm Zubie the amazing lightning bug.
I'm fast, I'm bright and I light up the
summer night. You can call me...
ZUPER ZUBIE !"

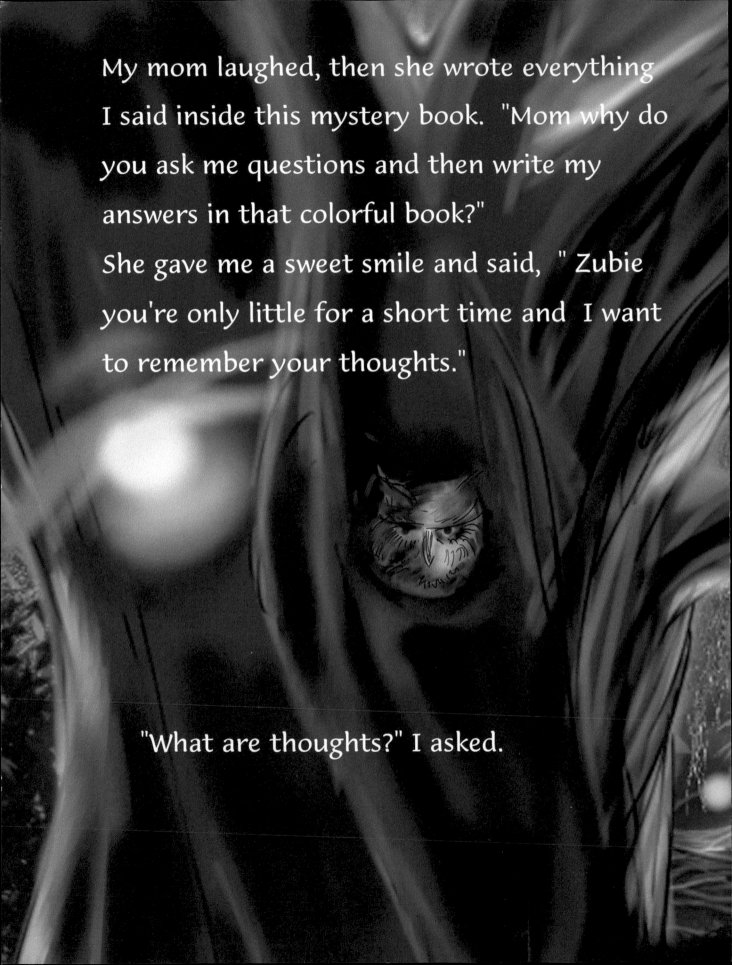

My mom laughed, then she wrote everything
I said inside this mystery book. "Mom why do
you ask me questions and then write my
answers in that colorful book?"

She gave me a sweet smile and said, " Zubie
you're only little for a short time and I want
to remember your thoughts."

"What are thoughts?" I asked.

"Thoughts are what you think, how you feel and how you see the world. You see you are going to grow up to be a big Zubie and you will have new feelings and new thoughts. I want to remember my little "Zuper Zubie" and the way you see the world today."

We hugged and I took off flying into the night.

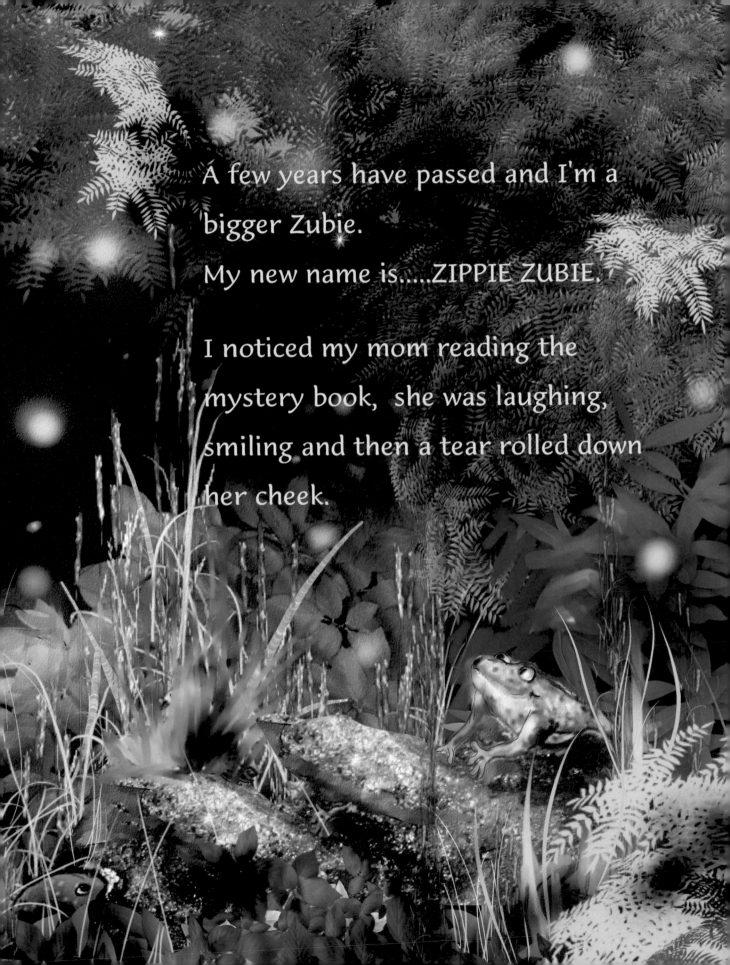

A few years have passed and I'm a
bigger Zubie.
My new name is.....ZIPPIE ZUBIE.

I noticed my mom reading the
mystery book, she was laughing,
smiling and then a tear rolled down
her cheek.

Mom, you're reading the mystery book, are you ok?"

"Oh Zubie, I've never been better.  This isn't a mystery book, it's a memory book.  Your memory book that we  created years ago.  I am so happy because I just visited your thoughts."

Once again we hugged and I flew into the night.

ZUBIE is here to help your parents make a memory book about you, so they can visit your wonderful thoughts when you get big like me.

Date:

All you have to do is answer
the questions on the Zubie
pages.  Have someone
write down your answers
the same way you say them.
Have fun!

What is your name?

Who is writing this down your answers?

Who is this memory book made for?

How old are you today?

Can you draw a picture of yourself below?

# Let's talk about your favorites:

What is your favorite number?

What is your favorite color?
(You can use crayons or markers to scribble them here.)

What is your favorite shape?
(Try drawing the shape here)

What is your favorite movie?

What is your favorite TV show?

What is your favorite song to sing?

What is your favorite book?

If you could go anywhere in the world,
where would you go?

How would you get there?

What would you take with you?

Can you describe outer space?

What would you bring with you into outer space?

What are angels?

Can you draw a picture of an angel?

What is your favorite thing to do before you go to bed every night?

What does it mean to have a dream?

Can you tell me one of your dreams?  If not, can you make one up?

Date:

Tell me about your family.
(mom, dad, brothers, sisters, grandparents)

What do you like about each of them?

What don't you like about them?

What do you love about them?

What is your favorite thing to do with each family member?

Describe your favorite toy:

Why is it your favorite toy?

Can you draw your favorite toy below?

What is your mom's favorite meal to eat?

How do you make that?

What is your dad's favorite meal to eat?

How do you make that?

Can you tell me what a treasure hunt is?

If you found a treasure chest, what would you like to be in it?

Can you draw  a treasure?

What does being healthy mean?


How do you stay healthy?

Can you tell me a time when you were happy?

Can you tell me a time when you were sad?

Can you tell me a time when you were angry?

Can you tell me a time when you were hurt?

Can you tell me a time when you were scared?

Can you tell me a time when you were proud?

Can you tell me a time when your mom and dad were proud of you?

What is love?

How does it feel?

What does it mean when you tell someone you love them?

Can you tell me a story that you made up?

Can you make up your own song?

If you could give your mom anything in the world what would it be?

If you could give your dad anything in the world what would it be?

How about your brothers or sisters or grandparents, what would you give them?

What is the most beautiful thing you have ever seen?

What is your favorite thing your mom has ever said to you?

What is your favorite thing your dad has ever said to you?

What makes you so special and so loved?